Louanne Pig in
The Talent Show

Louanne Pig in The Talent Show

Nancy Carlson

Carolrhoda Books, Inc. / Minneapolis

Carolrhoda Books, Inc.
A division of Lerner Publishing Group
241 First Avenue North
Minneapolis, MN 55401 U.S.A.

Website address: www.lernerbooks.com

Library of Congress Cataloging-in-Publication Data

Carlson, Nancy L.
      Louanne Pig in the talent show / by Nancy Carlson.
         p.   cm.
      Summary: No-talent Louanne's spirits droop as her friends prepare for the
talent show, but then she is called upon to perform in a very special way.
      ISBN-13: 978–1–57505–915–0 (lib. bdg. : alk. paper)
      ISBN-10: 1–57505–915–0 (lib. bdg. : alk. paper)
      [1. Talent shows—Fiction. 2. Pigs—Fiction. 3. Animals—Fiction.] I. Title.
Talent show. II. Title.
PZ7.C21665Lkm 2005
      [E]—dc22   2005003161

Manufactured in the United States of America
1 2 3 4 5 6 – JR – 10 09 08 07 06 05

To Mrs. Mansfield and Mrs. Blashfield,
two special teachers

Everyone was excited to try out for the annual talent show.

Everyone but Louanne, that is.
"I don't have any talent," she said.

"Why don't you try dancing," suggested Harriet.
"I can't dance," said Louanne.

"How about acrobatics," said Arnie.
"I know I could never do that," said Louanne.

"You could take up the tuba," suggested George.
"No way!" said Louanne.

"The flute, then," said Tony.
"I can't play *any* instruments," said Louanne.

"I'm going to sing a medley of Broadway tunes," said Ralph. "*Anyone* can sing."

"Not me," said Louanne. "I'm just a big no-talent dope!"

All week long, everywhere she went,

everyone was practicing.

"Who cares about a dumb old talent show anyway," Louanne muttered.

"I have better things to do."

Tryouts were held on Friday after school.
Harriet made it. Arnie made it. Tony made it.
Ralph made it. Even George made it, but not as a
tuba player.

George was going to be master of ceremonies.
"That's even better," he bragged. "I'll be on stage
ten times more than anyone else!"

"Talent shows are stupid," said Louanne,

and she buried herself in a book.

At last the big night arrived. Louanne thought of all her friends getting ready. She pictured the lights dimming, the curtain slowly rising. She felt miserable.

Suddenly the phone rang. It was Harriet. She was very upset.

"Louanne, you've just got to help us," she said. "George has laryngitis!"

"You mean you want *me* to be the master of
ceremonies?" asked Louanne.

"George has a wonderful costume," said Harriet.
"He says you can wear it. Pleeeease?"

But Louanne wasn't there to answer. She was
already on her way to the auditorium.

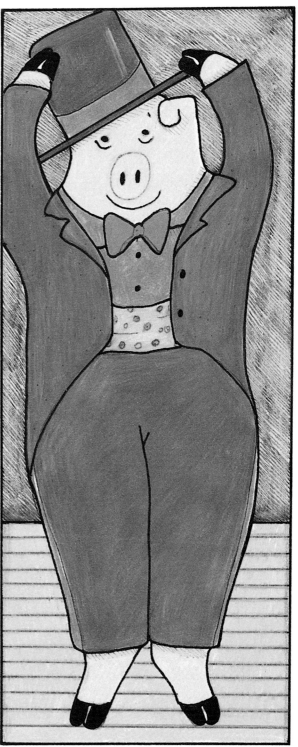

The evening was a great success.

"Still think talent shows are stupid?" asked Harriet.

"Who, *me*?" said Louanne.

"I LOVE show biz!"